WORLD'S
BEST
CHRISTMAS
STORIES

D0190027

Watermill Press

Table of Contents

The Gift of the Magi

O. HENRY

One dollar and eighty-seven cents. That was all. And sixty cents of it was in pennies. Pennies saved one and two at a time by bulldozing the grocer and the vegetable man and the butcher until one's cheeks burned with the silent imputation of parsimony that such close dealing implied. Three times Della counted it. One dollar and eighty-seven cents. And the next day would be Christmas.

There was clearly nothing to do but flop down on the shabby little couch and howl. So Della did it. Which instigates the moral reflection that life is made up of sobs, sniffles, and smiles, with sniffles predominating.

While the mistress of the home is gradually subsiding from the first stage to the second, take a look at the home. A furnished flat at $8 per week. It did not exactly beggar description, but it certainly had that word on the lookout for the mendicancy squad.

In the vestibule below was a mailbox into which no letter would go, and an electric button from which no mortal finger could coax a ring. Also appertaining thereunto was a card bearing the name "Mr. James Dillingham Young."

The "Dillingham" had been flung to the breeze during a former period of prosperity when its possessor was being paid $30 per week. Now, when the income was shrunk to $20, the letters of "Dillingham" looked blurred, as though they were thinking seriously of contracting a modest and unassuming D. But whenever Mr. Dillingham Young came home and reached his flat above, he was called "Jim" and greatly hugged by Mrs. James Dillingham Young, already introduced to you as Della. Which is all very good.

Della finished her cry and attended to her cheeks with the powder rag. She stood by the window and looked out dully at a gray cat walking a gray fence in a gray backyard. Tomorrow would be Christmas Day, and she had only $1.87 with which to buy Jim a present. She had been saving every penny she could for months, with this result. Twenty dollars a week doesn't go far. Expenses had been greater than she had calculated. They always are. Only $1.87 to buy a present for Jim. Her Jim. Many a happy hour she had spent planning for something nice for him. Something fine and rare and sterling—something just a little bit near to being worthy of the honor of being owned by Jim.

There was a pier-glass between the windows of the room. Perhaps you have seen a pier-glass in an $8 flat. A very thin and very agile person may, by observing his reflection in a rapid sequence of longitudinal strips, obtain a fairly accurate conception of his looks. Della, being slender, had mastered the art.

Suddenly she whirled from the window and stood before the glass. Her eyes were shining brilliantly, but her face had lost its color within twenty seconds. Rapidly she pulled down her hair and let it fall to its full length.

Now, there were two possessions of the James Dillingham Youngs in which they both took a mighty pride. One was Jim's gold watch that had been his father's and his grandfather's. The other was Della's hair. Had the Queen of Sheba lived in the flat across the airshaft, Della would have let her hair hang out the window some day to dry just to depreciate Her Majesty's jewels and gifts. Had King Solomon been the janitor, with all his treasures piled up in the basement, Jim would have pulled out his watch every time he passed, just to see him pluck at his beard from envy.

So now Della's beautiful hair fell about her rippling and shining like a cascade of brown waters. It reached below her knee and made itself almost a garment for her. And then she did it up again nervously and quickly. Once she faltered for a minute and stood still while a tear or two splashed on the worn red carpet.

On went her old brown jacket; on went her old brown hat. With a whirl of skirts and with the brilliant sparkle still in her eyes, she fluttered out the door and down the stairs to the street.

Where she stopped, the sign read: "Mme. Sofronie. Hair Goods of All Kinds." One flight up Della ran, and collected herself, panting. Madame, large, too white, chilly, hardly looked the "Sofronie."

"Will you buy my hair?" asked Della.

"I buy hair," said Madame. "Take ye hat off and let's have a sight at the looks of it."

Down rippled the brown cascade.

"Twenty dollars," said Madame, lifting the mass with a practiced hand.

"Give it to me quick," said Della.

Oh, the next two hours tripped by on rosy wings. Forget the hashed metaphor. She was ransacking the stores for Jim's present.

She found it at last. It surely had been made for Jim and no one else. There was no other like it in any of the stores, and she had turned all of them inside out. It was a platinum fob chain simple and chaste in design, properly proclaiming its value by substance alone and not by meretricious ornamentation—as all good things should do. It was even worthy of The Watch. As soon as she saw it she knew that it must be Jim's. It was like him. Quietness and value—the description applied to both. Twenty-one dollars they took from her for it, and she hurried home with the 87 cents. With that chain on his watch Jim might be properly anxious about the time in any company. Grand as the watch was, he sometimes looked at it on the sly on account of the old leather strap that he used in place of a chain.

When Della reached home her intoxication gave way a little to prudence and reason. She got out her curling irons and lighted the gas and went to work repairing the ravages made by generosity added to love. Which is always a tremendous task, dear friends— a mammoth task.

Within forty minutes her head was covered with tiny, close-lying curls that made her look wonderfully like a truant schoolboy. She looked at her reflection in the mirror long, carefully, and critically.

"If Jim doesn't kill me," she said to herself, "before he takes a second look at me, he'll say I look like a Coney Island chorus girl. But what could I do—oh! what could I do with a dollar and eighty-seven cents?"

At 7 o'clock the coffee was made and the frying pan was on the back of the stove and ready to cook the chops.

Jim was never late. Della doubled the fob chain in her hand and sat on the corner of the table near the door that he always entered. Then she heard his step on the stair away down on the first flight, and she turned white for just a moment. She had a habit of saying little silent prayers about the simplest everyday things, and now she whispered: "Please God, make him think I am still pretty."

The door opened and Jim stepped in and closed it. He looked thin and very serious. Poor fellow, he was only twenty two — and to be burdened with a family! He needed a new overcoat and he was without gloves.

Jim stopped inside the door, as immovable as a setter at the scent of quail. His eyes were fixed upon Della, and there was an expression in them that she could not read, and it terrified her. It was not anger, nor surprise, nor disapproval, nor horror, nor any of the sentiments that she had been prepared for. He simply stared at her fixedly with that peculiar expression on his face.

Della wriggled off the table and went for him.

"Jim, darling," she cried, "don't look at me that way. I had my hair cut off and sold it because I couldn't have lived through Christmas without giving you a present. It'll grow out again—you won't mind, will you? I just had to do it. My hair grows awfully fast. Say 'Merry Christmas!' Jim, and let's be happy. You don't know what a nice—what a beautiful, nice gift I've got for you."

"You've cut off your hair?" asked Jim, laboriously, as if he had not arrived at that patent fact yet even after the hardest mental labor.

"Cut it off and sold it," said Della. "Don't you like me just as well, anyhow? I'm me without my hair, ain't I?"

Jim looked about the room curiously.

"You say your hair is gone?" he said, with an air almost of idiocy.

"You needn't look for it," said Della. "It's sold, I tell you—sold and gone, too. It's Christmas Eve, boy. Be good to me, for it went for you. Maybe the hairs on my head were numbered," she went on with a sudden serious sweetness, "but nobody could ever count my love for you. Shall I put the chops on, Jim?"

Out of his trance Jim seemed quickly to wake. He enfolded his Della. For ten seconds let us regard with discreet scrutiny some inconsequential object in the other direction. Eight dollars a week or a million a year—what is the difference? A mathematician or a wit would give you the wrong answer. The magi brought valuable gifts, but that was not among them. This dark assertion will be illuminated later on.

Jim drew a package from his overcoat pocket and threw it upon the table.

"Don't make any mistake, Dell," he said, "about me. I don't think there's anything in the way of a haircut or a shave or a shampoo that could make me like my girl any less. But if you'll unwrap that package you may see why you had me going a while at first."

White fingers and nimble tore at the string and paper. And then an ecstatic scream of joy; and then, alas! a quick feminine change to hysterical tears and wails, necessitating the immediate employment of all the comforting powers of the lord of the flat.

For there lay The Combs—the set of combs, side and back, that Della had worshiped for long in a Broadway window. Beautiful combs, pure tortoise shell, with jeweled rims—just the shade to wear in the beautiful vanished hair. They were expensive combs, she knew, and her heart had simply craved and yearned over them without the least hope of possession. And now they were hers, but the tresses that should have adorned the coveted adornments were gone.

But she hugged them to her bosom, and at length she was able to look up with dim eyes and a smile and say: "My hair grows so fast, Jim!"

And then Della leaped up like a little singed cat and cried, "Oh, oh!"

Jim had not yet seen his beautiful present. She held it out to him eagerly upon her open palm. The dull precious metal seemed to flash with a reflection of her bright and ardent spirit.

"Isn't it a dandy, Jim? I hunted all over town to find it. You'll have to look at the time a hundred times a day now. Give me your watch. I want to see how it looks on it."

Instead of obeying, Jim tumbled down on the couch and put his hands under the back of his head and smiled.

"Dell," said he, "let's put our Christmas presents away and keep 'em a while. They're too nice to use just as presents. I sold the watch to get the money to buy your combs. And now suppose you put the chops on."

The magi, as you know, were wise men—wonderfully wise men—who brought gifts to the Babe in the manger. They invented the art of giving Christmas presents. Being wise, their gifts were no doubt wise ones, possibly bearing the privilege of exchange in case of duplication. And here I have lamely related to you the uneventful chronicle of two foolish children in a flat who most unwisely sacrificed for each other the greatest treasures of their house. But in a last word to the wise of these days let it be said that of all who give gifts these two were the wisest. Of all who give and receive gifts, such as they are wisest. Everywhere they are wisest. They are the magi.

A Christmas Dream and How It Came True

LOUISA MAY ALCOTT

"**I**'m so tired of Christmas I wish there never would be another one!" exclaimed a discontented-looking little girl, as she sat idly watching her mother arrange a pile of gifts two days before they were to be given.

"Why, Effie, what a dreadful thing to say! You are as bad as old Scrooge; and I'm afraid something will happen to you, as it did to him, if you don't care for dear Christmas," answered Mamma, almost dropping the silver horn she was filling with delicious candies.

"Who was Scrooge? What happened to him?" asked Effie, with a glimmer of interest in her listless face, as she picked out the sourest lemon-drop she could find; for nothing sweet suited her just then.

"He was one of Dickens's best people, and you can read the charming story some day. He hated Christmas until a strange dream showed him how dear and beautiful it was, and made a better man of him."

"I shall read it; for I like dreams, and have a great many curious ones myself. But they don't keep me from being tired of Christmas," said Effie, poking discontentedly among the sweeties for something worth eating.

"Why are you tired of what should be the happiest time of all the year?" asked Mamma, anxiously.

"Perhaps I shouldn't be if I had something new. But it is always the same, and there isn't any more surprise about it. I always find heaps of goodies in my stocking. Don't like some of them, and soon get tired of those I do like. We always have a great dinner, and I eat too much, and feel ill next day. Then there is a Christmas tree somewhere, with a doll on top, or a stupid old Santa Claus, and children dancing and screaming over bonbons and toys that break, and shiny things that are of no use. Really, Mamma, I've had so many Christmases all alike that I don't think I can bear another one." And Effie laid herself flat on the sofa, as if the mere idea was too much for her.

Her mother laughed at her despair, but was sorry to see her little girl so discontented, when she had everything to make her happy, and had known but ten Christmas days.

"Suppose we don't give you any presents at all—how would that suit you?" asked Mamma, anxious to please her spoiled child.

"I should like one large and splendid one, and one dear little one, to remember some very nice person by," said Effie, who was a fanciful little body, full of odd whims and notions, which her friends loved to gratify, regardless of time, trouble, or money; for she was the last of three little girls, and very dear to all the family.

"Well, my darling, I will see what I can do to please you, and not say a word until all is ready. If I could only get a new idea to start with!" And Mamma went on tying up her pretty bundles with a thoughtful face, while Effie strolled to the window to watch the rain that kept her indoors and made her dismal.

"Seems to me poor children have better times than rich ones. I can't go out, and there is a girl about my age splashing along, without any maid to fuss about rubbers and cloaks and umbrellas and colds. I wish I was a beggar-girl."

"Would you like to be hungry, cold, and ragged, to beg all day, and sleep on an ash-heap at night?" asked Mamma, wondering what would come next.

"Cinderella did, and had a nice time in the end. This girl out here has a basket of scraps on her arm, and a big old shawl all around her, and doesn't seem to care a bit, though the water runs out of the toes of her boots. She goes paddling along, laughing at the rain, and eating a cold potato as if it tasted nicer than the chicken and ice cream I had for dinner. Yes, I do think poor children are happier than rich ones."

"So do I, sometimes. At the Orphan Asylum today I saw two dozen merry little souls who have no parents, no home, and no hope of Christmas beyond a stick of candy or a cake. I wish you had been there to see how happy they were, playing with the old toys some richer children had sent them."

"You may give them all mine; I'm so tired of them I never want to see them again," said Effie, turning from the window to the pretty doll house full of everything a child's heart could desire.

"I will, and let you begin again with something you will not tire of, if I can only find it." And Mamma knit her brows trying to discover some grand surprise for this child who didn't care for Christmas.

Nothing more was said then; and wandering off to the library, Effie found "A Christmas Carol," and, curling herself up in the sofa corner, read it all before tea. Some of it she did not understand; but she laughed and cried over many parts of the charming story, and felt better without knowing why.

All the evening she thought of poor Tiny Tim, Mrs. Cratchit with the pudding, and the stout old gentleman who danced so gayly that "his legs twinkled in the air." Presently bedtime arrived.

"Come now, and toast your feet," said Effie's nurse, "while I do your pretty hair and tell stories."

"I'll have a fairy tale tonight, a very interesting one," commanded Effie, as she put on her blue silk wrapper and little fur-lined slippers to sit before the fire and have her long curls brushed.

So Nursey told her best tales; and when at last the child lay down under her lace curtains, her head was full of a curious jumble of Christmas elves, poor children, snowstorms, sugarplums, and surprises. So it is no wonder that she dreamed all night; and this was the dream, which she never quite forgot.

She found herself sitting on a stone, in the middle of a great field, all alone. The snow was falling fast, a bitter wind whistled by, and night was coming on. She felt hungry, cold, and tired, and did not know where to go nor what to do.

"I wanted to be a beggar-girl, and now I am one; but I don't like it, and wish somebody would come and take care of me. I don't know who I am, and I think I must be lost," thought Effie, with the curious interest one takes in oneself in dreams.

But the more she thought about it, the more bewildered she felt. Faster fell the snow, colder blew the wind, darker grew the night; and poor Effie made up her mind that she was quite forgotten and left to freeze alone. The tears were chilled on her cheeks, her feet felt like icicles, and her heart died within her, so hungry, frightened, and forlorn was she. Laying her head on her knees, she gave herself up for lost, and sat there with the great flakes fast turning her to a little white mound, when suddenly the sound of music reached her, and starting up, she looked and listened with all her eyes and ears.

Far away a dim light shone, and a voice was heard singing. She tried to run toward the welcome glimmer, but could not stir, and stood like a small statue of expectation while the light drew nearer, and the sweet words of the song grew clearer.

"From our happy home
Through the world we roam
One week in all the year,
Making winter spring
With the joy we bring
For Christmas-tide is here.

"Now the eastern star
Shines from afar
To light the poorest home;
Hearts warmer grow,
Gifts freely flow,
For Christmas-tide has come.

"Now gay trees rise
Before young eyes,
Abloom with tempting cheer;
Blithe voices sing.
And blithe bells ring,
For Christmas-tide is here.

"Oh, happy chime,
Oh, blessed time,

That draws us all so near!
'Welcome, dear day,'
All creatures say,
For Christmas-tide is here."

A child's voice sang, a child's hand carried the little candle; and in the circle of soft light it shed, Effie saw a pretty child coming to her through the night and snow. A rosy, smiling creature, wrapped in white fur, with a wreath of green and scarlet holly on its shining hair, the magic candle in one hand, and the other outstretched as if to shower gifts and warmly press all other hands.

Effie forgot to speak as this bright vision came nearer, leaving no trace of footsteps in the snow, only lighting the way with its little candle, and filling the air with the music of its song.

"Dear child, you are lost, and I have come to find you," said the stranger, taking Effie's cold hands in his, with a smile like sunshine, while every holly berry glowed like a little fire.

"Do you know me?" asked Effie, feeling no fear, but a great gladness, at his coming.

"I know all children, and go to find them; for this is my holiday, and I gather them from all parts of the world to be merry with me once a year."

"Are you an angel?" asked Effie, looking for the wings.

"No; I am a Christmas spirit, and live with my friends in a pleasant place, getting ready for our holiday, when we are let out to roam about the world, helping to make this a happy time for all who will let us in. Will you come and see how we work?"

"I will go anywhere with you. Don't leave me again," cried Effie, gladly.

"First I will make you comfortable. That is what we love to do. You are cold, and you shall be warm; hungry, and I will feed you; sorrowful, and I will make you gay."

With a wave of his candle all three miracles were wrought—for the snowflakes turned to a white fur cloak and hood on Effie's head and shoulders; a bowl of hot soup came sailing to her lips, and vanished when she had eagerly drunk the last drop; and suddenly the dismal field changed to a new world so full of wonders that all her troubles were forgotten in a minute.

Bells were ringing so merrily that it was hard to keep from dancing. Green garlands hung on the walls, and every tree was a Christmas tree full of toys, and blazing with candles that never went out.

In one place many little spirits sewed like mad on warm clothes, turning off work faster than any sewing machine ever invented, and great piles were made ready to be sent to poor people. Other busy creatures packed money into purses, and wrote checks which they sent flying away on the wind—a lovely kind of snowstorm to fall into a world below full of poverty.

Older and graver spirits were looking over piles of little books, in which the records of the past year were kept, telling how different people had spent it, and what sort of gifts they deserved. Some got peace, some disappointment, some remorse and sorrow, some great joy and hope. The rich had generous thoughts sent them; the poor, gratitude and contentment. Children had more love and duty to parents; and parents renewed patience, wisdom, and satisfaction for and in their children. No one was forgotten.

"Please tell me what splendid place this is?" asked Effie, as soon as she could collect her wits after the first look at all these astonishing things.

"This is the Christmas world; and here we work all the year round, never tired of getting ready for the happy day. See, these are the saints just setting off, for some have far to go, and the children must not be disappointed."

As he spoke the spirit pointed to four gates, out of which four great sleighs were just driving, laden with toys, while a jolly old Santa Claus sat in the middle of each, drawing on his mittens and tucking up his wraps for a long cold drive.

"Why, I thought there was only one Santa Claus, and even he was a humbug," cried Effie, astonished at the sight.

"Never give up your faith in the sweet old stories, even after you come to see that they are only the pleasant shadow of a lovely truth."

Just then the sleighs went off with a great jingling of bells and pattering of reindeer hoofs, while all the spirits gave a cheer that was heard in the lower world, where people said, "Hear the stars sing."

"I never will say there isn't any Santa Claus again. Now, show me more."

"You will like to see this place, I think, and may learn something here perhaps."

The spirit smiled as he led the way to a little door, through which Effie peeped into a world of dolls. Doll houses were in full blast, with dolls of all sorts going on like live people. Waxed ladies sat in their parlors elegantly dressed; some dolls cooked in the kitchens; nurses walked out with the bits of dollies; and the streets were full of tin soldiers marching, wooden horses prancing, express wagons rumbling; and little men hurrying to and fro. Shops were there, and tiny people buying legs of mutton, pounds of tea, mites of clothes, and everything dolls use or wear or want.

But presently she saw that in some ways the dolls improved upon the manners and customs of human beings, and she watched eagerly to learn why they did these things. A fine Paris doll driving in her carriage took up another doll who was hobbling along with a basket of clean clothes, and carried her to her journey's end, as if it were the proper thing to do. Another interesting china lady took off her comfortable red cloak and put it around a poor wooden creature done up in a paper shift, and so badly painted that its face would have sent some babies into fits.

"Seems to me I once knew a rich girl who didn't give her things to poor girls. I wish I could remember who she was, and tell her to be as kind as that china doll," said Effie, much touched at the sweet way the pretty creature wrapped up the poor fright, and then ran off in her little gray gown to buy a shiny fowl stuck on a wooden platter for her invalid mother's dinner.

"We recall these things to people's minds by dreams. I think the girl you speak of won't forget this one." And the spirit smiled, as if he enjoyed some joke which she did not see.

A little bell rang as she looked, and away scampered the children into the red-and-green schoolhouse with the roof that lifted up, so one could see how nicely they sat at their desks with mites of books, or drew on the inch-square blackboards with crumbs of chalk.

"They know their lessons very well, and are as still as mice. We make a great racket at our school, and get bad marks every day. I shall tell the girls they had better mind what they do, or their dolls will be better scholars than they are," said Effie, much impressed, as she peeped in and saw no rod in the hand of the little mistress, who looked up and shook her head at the intruder, as if begging her to go away before the order of the school was disturbed.

Effie retired at once, but could not resist one look in the window of a fine mansion, where the family were at dinner, the children behaved so well at the table, and never grumbled a bit when their mamma said they could not have any more fruit.

"Now, show me something else," she said, as they came again to the low door that led out of Doll-land.

"You have seen how we prepare for Christmas; let me show you where we love best to send our good and happy gifts," answered the spirit, giving her his hand again.

"I know. I've seen ever so many," began Effie, thinking of her own Christmases.

"No, you have never seen what I will show you. Come away, and remember what you see tonight."

Like a flash that bright world vanished, and Effie found herself in a part of the city she had never seen before. It was far away from the gayer places, where every store was brilliant with lights and full of pretty things, and every house wore a festival air, while people hurried to and fro with merry greetings. It was down among the dingy streets where the poor lived, and where there was no making ready for Christmas.

Hungry women looked in at the shabby shops, longing to buy meat and bread, but empty pockets forbade. Tipsy men drank up their wages in the barrooms; and in many cold dark chambers little children huddled under the thick blankets, trying to forget their misery in sleep.

No nice dinners filled the air with savory smells, no gay trees dropped toys and bonbons into eager hands, no little stockings hung in rows beside the chimneypiece ready to be filled, no happy sounds of music, gay voices, and dancing feet were heard; and there were no signs of Christmas anywhere.

"Don't they have any in this place?" asked Effie, shivering, as she held fast the spirit's hand, following where he led her.

"We come to bring it. Let me show you our best workers." And the spirit pointed to some sweet-faced men and women who came stealing into the poor houses, working such beautiful miracles that Effie could only stand and watch.

Some slipped money into the empty pockets, and sent happy mothers to buy all the comforts they needed; others led the drunken men out of temptation, and took them home to find safer pleasures there. Fires were kindled on cold hearths, tables spread as if by magic, and warm clothes wrapped around shivering limbs. Flowers suddenly bloomed in the chambers of the sick; old people found themselves remembered; sad hearts were consoled by a tender word, and wicked ones softened by the story of Him who forgave all sin.

But the sweetest work was for the children; and Effie held her breath to watch these human fairies hang up and fill the little stockings without which a child's Christmas is not perfect, putting in things that once she would have thought very humble presents, but which now seemed beautiful and precious because these poor babies had nothing.

"That is so beautiful! I wish I could make merry Christmas as these good people do, and be loved and thanked as they are," said Effie, softly, as she watched the busy men and women do their work and steal away without thinking of any reward but their own satisfaction.

"You can if you will. I have shown you the way. Try it, and see how happy your own holiday will be hereafter."

As he spoke, the spirit seemed to put his arms about her, and vanished with a kiss.

"Oh, stay and show me more!" cried Effie, trying to hold him fast.

"Darling, wake up, and tell me why you are smiling in your sleep," said a voice in her ear; and opening her eyes, there was Mamma bending over her, and morning sunshine streaming into the room.

"Are they all gone? Did you hear the bells? Wasn't it splendid?" she asked, rubbing her eyes, and looking about her for the pretty child who was so real and sweet.

"You have been dreaming at a great rate—talking in your sleep, laughing, and clapping your hands as if you were cheering someone. Tell me what was so splendid," said Mamma, soothing the tumbled hair and lifting up the sleepy head.

Then, while she was being dressed, Effie told her dream, and

Nursey thought it very wonderful; but Mamma smiled to see how curiously things the child had thought, read, heard, and seen through the day were mixed up in her sleep.

"The spirit said I could work lovely miracles if I tried; but I don't know how to begin, for I have no magic candle to make feasts appear, and light up groves of Christmas trees, as he did," said Effie, sorrowfully.

"Yes you have. We will do it! we will do it!" And clapping her hands, Mamma suddenly began to dance all over the room as if she had lost her wits.

"How? how? You must tell me, Mamma," cried Effie, dancing after her, and ready to believe anything possible when she remembered the adventures of the past night.

"I've got it! I've got it!—the new idea. A splendid one, if I can only carry it out!" And Mamma waltzed the little girl around till her curls flew wildly in the air, while Nursey laughed as if she would die.

"Tell me! tell me!" shrieked Effie.

"No, no; it is a surprise—a grand surprise for Christmas day!" sung Mamma, evidently charmed with her happy thought. "Now, come to breakfast; for we must work like bees if we want to play spirits tomorrow. You and Nursey will go out shopping, and get heaps of things, while I arrange matters behind the scenes."

They were running downstairs as Mamma spoke, and Effie called out breathlessly—

"It won't be a surprise; for I know you are going to ask some poor children here, and have a tree or something. It won't be like my dream; for they had ever so many trees, and more children than we can find anywhere."

"There will be no tree, no party, no dinner, in this house at all, and no presents for you. Won't that be a surprise?" And Mamma laughed at Effie's bewildered face.

"Do it. I shall like it, I think; and I won't ask any questions, so it will all burst upon me when the time comes," she said; and she ate her breakfast thoughtfully, for this really would be a new sort of Christmas.

All that morning Effie trotted after Nursey in and out of shops, buying dozens of barking dogs, wooly lambs, and squeaking birds; tiny tea sets, gay picture books, mittens and hoods, dolls and candy. Parcel after parcel was sent home; but when Effie returned she saw no trace of them, though she peeped everywhere. Nursey chuckled, but wouldn't give a hint, and went out again in the afternoon with a long list of more things to buy; while Effie wandered forlornly about the house, missing the usual merry stir that went before the Christmas dinner and the evening fun.

As for Mamma, she was quite invisible all day, and came in at night so tired that she could only lie on the sofa to rest, smiling as if some very pleasant thought made her happy in spite of weariness.

"Is the surprise going on all right?" asked Effie, anxiously; for it seemed an immense time to wait till another evening came.

"Beautifully! Better than I expected; for several of my good friends are helping, or I couldn't have done as I wish. I know you will like it, dear, and long remember this new way of making Christmas merry."

Mamma gave her a very tender kiss, and Effie went to bed.

***

The next day was a very strange one; for when she woke there was no stocking to examine, no pile of gifts under her napkin, no one said, "Merry Christmas!" to her, and the dinner was just as usual to her. Mamma vanished again, and Nursey kept wiping her eyes and saying: "The dear things! It's the prettiest idea I ever heard of. No one but your blessed ma could have done it."

"Do stop, Nursey, or I shall go crazy because I don't know the secret!" cried Effie, more than once; and she kept her eye on the clock, for at seven in the evening the surprise was to come off.

The longed-for hour arrived at last, and the child was too excited to ask questions when Nursey put on her cloak and hood, led her to the carriage, and they drove away, leaving their house the one dark and silent one in the row.

"I feel like the girls in the fairy tales who are led off to strange places and see fine things," said Effie, in a whisper, as they jingled through the gay streets.

"Ah, my deary, it *is* like a fairy tale, I do assure you, and you will see finer things than most children will tonight. Steady, now, and do just as I tell you, and don't say one word whatever you see," answered Nursey, quite quivering with excitement as she patted a large box in her lap, and nodded and laughed with twinkling eyes.

They drove into a dark yard, and Effie was led through a back door to a little room, where Nursey coolly proceeded to take off not only Effie's cloak and hood but her dress and shoes also. Effie stared and bit her lips, but kept still until out of the box came a little white fur coat and boots, a wreath of holly leaves and berries, and a candle with a frill of gold paper around it. A long "Oh!" escaped her then; and when she was dressed and saw herself in the glass, she started back, exclaiming, "Why, Nursey, I look like the spirit in my dream!"

"So you do; and that's the part you are to play, my pretty! Now whist, while I blind your eyes and put you in your place."

"Shall I be afraid?" whispered Effie, full of wonder; for as they went out she heard the sound of many voices, the tramp of many feet, and, in spite of the bandage, was sure a great light shone upon her when she stopped.

"You needn't be; I shall stand close by, and your ma will be there."

After the handkerchief was tied about her eyes, Nursey led Effie up some steps, and placed her on a high platform, where something like leaves touched her head, and the soft snap of lamps seemed to fill the air.

Music began as soon as Nursey clapped her hands, the voices outside sounded nearer, and the tramp was evidently coming up the stairs.

"Now, my precious, look and see how you and your dear ma have made a merry Christmas for them that needed it!"

Off went the bandage; and for a minute Effie really did think she was asleep again, for she actually stood in "a grove of Christmas trees," all gay and shining as in her vision. Twelve on a side, in two rows down the room, stood the little pines, each on its low table and behind Effie a taller one rose to the roof, hung with wreaths of popcorn, apples, oranges, horns of candy, and cakes of all sorts, from sugary hearts to gingerbread Jumbos. On the smaller trees she saw many of her own discarded toys and those Nursey bought, as well as heaps that seemed to have rained down straight from that delightful Christmas country where she felt as if she was again.

"How splendid! Who is it for? What is that noise? Where is Mamma?" cried Effie, pale with pleasure and surprise, as she stood looking down the brilliant little street from her high place.

Before Nursey could answer, the doors at the lower end flew open, and in marched twenty-four little blue-gowned orphan girls, singing sweetly, until amazement changed the song to cries of joy and wonder as the shining spectacle appeared. While they stood staring with round eyes at the wilderness of pretty things about them, Mamma stepped up beside Effie, and holding her hand fast to give her courage, told the story of the dream in a few simple words, ending in this way:

"So my little girl wanted to be a Christmas spirit too, and make this a happy day for those who had not as many pleasures and comforts as she has. She likes surprises, and we planned this for you all. She shall play the good fairy, and give each of you something from this tree, after which everyone will find her own name on a small tree, and can go to enjoy it in her own way. March by, my dears, and let us fill your hands."

Nobody told them to do it, but all the hands were clapped heartily before a single child stirred; then one by one they came to look up wonderingly at the pretty giver of the feast as she leaned down to offer them great yellow oranges, red apples, bunches of grapes, bonbons, and cakes, till all were gone, and a double row of smiling faces turned toward her as the children filed back to their places in the orderly way they had been taught.

Then each was led to her own tree by the good ladies who had helped Mamma with all their hearts; and the happy hubbub that arose would have satisfied even Santa Claus himself—shrieks of joy, dances of delight, laughter and tears (for some tender little things could not bear so much pleasure at once, and sobbed with mouths full of candy and hands full of toys). How they ran to show one another the new treasures! how they peeped and tasted, pulled and pinched, until the air was full of queer noises, the floor covered with papers, and the little trees left bare of all but candles!

"I don't think heaven can be any gooder than this," sighed one small girl, as she looked about her in a blissful maze, holding her full apron with one hand, while she luxuriously carried sugarplums to her mouth with the other.

"Is that a truly angel up there?" asked another, fascinated by the little white figure with the wreath on its shining hair, who in some mysterious way had been the cause of all this merry-making.

"I wish I dared to go and kiss her for this splendid party," said a lame child, leaning on her crutch, as she stood near the steps, wondering how it seemed to sit in a mother's lap, as Effie was doing, while she watched the happy scene before her.

Effie heard her, and remembering Tiny Tim, ran down and put her arms about the pale child, kissing the wistful face, as she said sweetly, "You may; but Mamma deserves the thanks. She did it all; I only dreamed about it."

Lame Katy felt as if "a truly angel" was embracing her, and could only stammer out her thanks, while the other children ran to see the pretty spirit, and touch her soft dress, until she stood in a crowd of blue gowns laughing as they held up their gifts for her to see and admire.

Mamma leaned down and whispered one word to the older girls; and suddenly they all took hands to dance around Effie, singing as they skipped.

It was a pretty sight, and the ladies found it hard to break up the happy revel; but it was late for small people, and too much fun is a mistake. So the girls fell into line, and marched before Effie and Mamma again, to say good night with such grateful little faces that the eyes of those who looked grew dim with tears. Mamma kissed every one; and many a hungry childish heart felt as if the touch of those tender lips was their best gift. Effie shook so many small hands that her own tingled; and when Katy came she pressed a small doll into Effie's hand, whispering, "You didn't have a single present, and we had lots. Do keep that; it's the prettiest thing I got."

"I will," answered Effie, and held it fast until the last smiling face was gone; the surprise all over, and she safe in her own bed, too tired and happy for anything but sleep.

"Mamma, it *was* a beautiful surprise, and I thank you so much! I don't see how you ever did it; but I like it best of all the Christmases I ever had, and mean to make one every year. I had my splendid big present, and here is the dear little one to keep for love of poor Katy; so even that part of my wish came true."

And Effie fell asleep with a happy smile on her lips, her one humble gift still in her hand, and a new love for Christmas in her heart that never changed through a long life spent in doing good.

The Little Match Girl

HANS CHRISTIAN ANDERSEN

It was terribly cold; it snowed and was already almost dark, and evening came on, the last evening of the year. In the cold and gloom a poor little girl, bareheaded and barefoot, was walking through the streets. When she left her own house she certainly had had slippers on, but of what use were they? They were very big slippers, and her mother had used them till then, so big were they. The little maid lost them as she slipped across the road, where two carriages were rattling by terribly fast. One slipper was not to be found again, and a boy had seized the other and run away with it. He thought he could use it very well as a cradle some day when he had children of his own. So now the little girl went with her little naked feet, which were quite red and blue with the cold. In an old apron she carried a number of matches, and a bundle of them in her hand. No one had bought anything of her all day, and no one had given her a farthing.

Shivering with cold and hunger, she crept along, a picture of misery, poor little girl! The snowflakes covered her long fair hair, which fell in pretty curls over her neck; but she did not think of that now. In all the windows lights were shining, and there was a glorious smell of roast goose, for it was New Year's Eve. Yes, she thought of that!

In a corner formed by two houses, one of which projected beyond the other, she sat down, cowering. She had drawn up her little feet, but she was still colder, and she did not dare to go home, for she had sold no matches and did not bring a farthing of money. From her father she would certainly receive a beating; and, besides, it was cold at home, for they had nothing over them but a roof through which the wind whistled, though the largest holes had been stopped with straw and rags.

Her little hands were almost benumbed with the cold. Ah, a match might do her good, if she could only draw one from the bundle and rub it against the wall and warm her hands at it. She drew one out. R-r-atch! how it sputtered and burned! It was a warm, bright flame, like a little candle, when she held her hands over it; it was a wonderful little light! It really seemed to the little girl as if she sat before a great polished stove with bright brass feet and a brass cover. How the fire burned! How comfortable it was! But the little flame went out, the stove vanished, and she had only the remains of the burnt match in her hand.

A second was rubbed against the wall. It burned up, and when the light fell upon the wall it became transparent like a thin veil, and she could see through it into the room. On the table a snow-white cloth was spread; upon it stood a shining dinner service; the roast goose smoked gloriously, stuffed with apples and dried plums. And, what was still more splendid to behold, the goose hopped down from the dish and waddled along the floor, with a knife and fork in its breast, to the little girl. Then the match went out and only the thick, damp, cold wall was before her. She lighted another match. Then she was sitting under a beautiful Christmas tree; it was greater and more ornamented than the one she had seen through the glass door at the rich merchant's. Thousands of candles burned upon the green branches, and colored pictures like those in the print shops looked down upon them. The little girl stretched forth her hand toward them; then the match went out. The Christmas lights mounted higher. She saw them now as stars in the sky; one of them fell down, forming a long line of fire.

"Now someone is dying," thought the little girl, for her old grandmother, the only person who had loved her, and who was now dead, had told her that when a star fell down a soul mounted up to God.

She rubbed another match against the wall; it became bright again, and in the brightness the old grandmother stood clear and shining, mild and lovely.

"Grandmother!" cried the child. "Oh, take me with you! I know you will go when the match is burned out. You will vanish like the warm fire, the warm food, and the great, glorious Christmas tree!"

And she hastily rubbed the whole bundle of matches, for she wished to hold her grandmother fast. And the matches burned with such a glow that it became brighter than in the middle of the day; grandmother had never been so large or so beautiful. She took the little girl in her arms, and both flew in brightness and joy above the earth, very, very high, and up there was neither cold, nor hunger, nor care—they were with God.

But in the corner, leaning against the wall, sat the poor girl with red cheeks and smiling mouth, frozen to death on the last evening of the old year. The New Year's sun rose upon a little corpse! The child sat there, stiff and cold, with the matches, of which one bundle was burned. "She wanted to warm herself," the people said. No one imagined what a beautiful thing she had seen and in what glory she had gone in with her grandmother to the New Year's Day.

Christmas at Mole End

KENNETH GRAHAME

"What a capital little house this is!" Mr. Rat called out cheerily. "So compact! So well planned! Everything here and everything in its place! We'll make a jolly night of it. The first thing we want is a good fire; I'll see to that—I always know where to find things. So this is the parlor? Splendid! Your own idea, those little sleeping bunks in the wall? Capital! Now, I'll fetch the wood and the coals, and you get a duster, Mole—you'll find one in the drawer of the kitchen—and try and smarten things up a bit. Bustle about, old chap!"

Encouraged by his inspiriting companion, the Mole roused himself and dusted and polished with energy and heartiness, while Rat, running to and fro with armfuls of fuel, soon had a

32

cheerful blaze roaring up the chimney. He hailed the Mole to come and warm himself; but Mole promptly had another fit of the blues, dropping down on a couch in dark despair and burying his face in his duster.

"Rat," he moaned, "how about your supper, you poor, cold, hungry, weary animal? I've nothing to give you—nothing—not a crumb!"

"What a fellow you are for giving in!" said the Rat reproachfully. "Why, only just now I saw a sardine-opener on the kitchen dresser, quite distinctly; and everybody knows that means there are sardines about somewhere in the neighborhood. Rouse yourself! pull yourself together, and come with me and forage."

They went and foraged accordingly, hunting through every cupboard and turning out every drawer. The result was not so very depressing after all, though of course it might have been better; a tin of sardines—a box of captain's biscuits, nearly full—and a German sausage encased in silver paper.

"There's a banquet for you!" observed the Rat, as he arranged the table. "I know some animals who would give their ears to be sitting down to supper with us tonight!"

"No bread!" groaned the Mole dolorously; "no butter, no—"

"No *pâté de foie gras,* no champagne!" continued the Rat, grinning. "And that reminds me—what's that little door at the end of the passage? Your cellar, of course! Every luxury in this house! Just you wait a minute."

He made for the cellar door, and presently reappeared somewhat dusty, with a bottle of cider in each paw and another under each arm. "Self-indulgent beggar you seem to be, Mole," he observed. "Deny yourself nothing. This is really the jolliest little place I ever was in. Now, wherever did you pick up those prints? Make the placc look so home-like, they do. No wonder you're so fond of it, Mole. Tell us all about it, and how you came to make it what it is."

Then, while the Rat busied himself fetching plates, and knives and forks, and mustard which he mixed in an egg-cup, the Mole, his bosom still heaving with the stress of his recent emotion, related—somewhat shyly at first, but with more freedom as he warmed to his subject—how this was planned, and how that was thought out, and how this was got through a windfall from an aunt, and that was a wonderful find and a bargain, and this other thing was bought out of laborious savings and a certain amount of "going without." His spirits finally quite restored, he must needs go and caress his possessions, and take a lamp and show off their points to his visitor, and expatiate on them, quite forgetful of the supper they both so much needed; Rat, who was desperately hungry but strove to conceal it, nodding seriously, examining with a puckered brow, and saying "Wonderful," and "Most remarkable," at intervals, when the chance for an observation was given him.

At last the Rat succeeded in decoying him to the table, and had just got seriously to work with the sardine-opener when sounds were heard from the forecourt without—sounds like the scuffling of small feet in the gravel and a confused murmur of tiny voices, while broken sentences reached them—"Now, all in a line—hold the lantern up a bit, Tommy—clear your throats first—no coughing after I say one, two, three.—Where's young Bill?—Here, come on, do, we're all a-waiting—"

"What's up?" inquired the Rat, pausing in his labors.

"I think it must be the field mice," replied the Mole, with a touch of pride in his manner. "They go around carol-singing regularly at this time of the year. They're quite an institution in these parts. And they never pass me over—they come to Mole End last of all; and I used to give them hot drinks, and supper too sometimes, when I could afford it. It will be like old times to hear them again."

"Let's have a look!" cried the Rat, jumping up and running to the door.

It was a pretty sight, and a seasonable one, that met their

eyes when they flung the door open. In the forecourt, lit by the dim rays of a horn lantern, some eight or ten little field mice stood in a semicircle, red worsted comforters around their throats, their forepaws thrust deep into their pockets, their feet jigging for warmth. With bright beady eyes they glanced shyly at each other, sniggering a little, sniffing and applying coat-sleeves a good deal. As the door opened, one of the elder ones that carried the lantern was just saying, "Now then, one, two, three!" and forthwith their shrill little voices uprose on the air, singing one of the old-time carols that their forefathers composed in fields that were fallow and held by frost, or when snow-bound in chimney corners, and handed down to be sung in the miry street to lamplit windows.

Carol

Villagers all, this frosty tide,
Let your doors swing open wide,
Though wind may follow, and snow beside,
Yet draw us in by your fire to bide;
Joy shall be yours in the morning!

Here we stand in the cold and the sleet,
Blowing fingers and stamping feet,
Come from far away you to greet—
You by the fire and we in the street—
Bidding you joy in the morning!

For ere one half of the night was gone,
Sudden a star has led us on,
Raining bliss and benison—
Bliss tomorrow and more anon,
Joy for every morning!

Goodman Joseph toiled through the snow—
Saw the star o'er a stable low;
Mary she might not further go—
Welcome thatch, and little below!
  Joy was hers in the morning.

And then they heard the angels tell
"Who were the first to cry Noel?
Animals all, as it befell,
In the stable where they did dwell!
  Joy shall be theirs in the morning!"

The voices ceased, the singers, bashful but smiling, exchanged sidelong glances, and silence succeeded—but for a moment only. Then, from up above and far away, down the tunnel they had so lately traveled was borne to their ears in a faint musical hum the sound of distant bells ringing a joyful and clangorous peal.

"Very well sung, boys!" cried the Rat heartily. "And now come along in, all of you, and warm yourselves by the fire, and have something hot!"

"Yes, come along, field mice," cried the Mole eagerly. "This is quite like old times! Shut the door after you. Pull up that settle to the fire. Now, you just wait a minute, while we— O, Ratty!" he cried in despair, plumping down on a seat, with tears impending. "Whatever are we doing? We've nothing to give them!"

"You leave all that to me," said the masterful Rat. "Here, you with the lantern! Come over this way. I want to talk to you. Now, tell me, are there any shops open at this hour of the night?"

"Why, certainly, sir," replied the field mouse respectfully. "At this time of the year our shops keep open to all sorts of hours."

"Then look here!" said the Rat. "You go off at once, you and your lantern, and you get me—"

Here much muttered conversation ensued, and the Mole only heard bits of it, such as—"Fresh, mind!—no, a pound of that will do—see you get Buggins's, for I won't have any other—no, only the best—if you can't get it there, try somewhere else—yes, of course, homemade, no tinned stuff—well then, do the best you can!" Finally, there was a chink of coin passing from paw to paw, the field mouse was provided with an ample basket for his purchases, and off he hurried, he and his lantern.

The rest of the field mice, perched in a row on the settle, their small legs swinging, gave themselves up to the enjoyment of the fire, and toasted their chilblains till they tingled; while the Mole, failing to draw them into easy conversation, plunged into family history and made each of them recite the names of his numerous brothers, who were too young, it appeared, to be allowed to go out a-caroling this year, but looked forward very shortly to winning the parental consent.

The Rat, meanwhile, was busy examining the label on one of the cider bottles. "I perceive this to be Old Burton," he remarked approvingly. "Sensible Mole! The very thing! Now we shall be able to heat up some cider! Get the things ready, Mole, while I draw the corks."

It did not take long to prepare the brew and thrust the tin heater well into the red heart of the fire; and soon every field mouse was forgetting he had ever been cold in all his life.

"They act plays too, these fellows," the Mole explained to the Rat. "Make them up all by themselves, and act them afterward. And very well they do it, too! They gave us a capital one last year, about a field mouse who was captured at sea by a Barbary corsair, and made to row in a galley; and when he escaped and got home again, his lady-love had gone into a convent. Here, you! You were in it, I remember. Get up and recite a bit."

The field mouse addressed got up on his legs, giggled shyly, looked around the room, and remained absolutely tongue-tied.

His comrades cheered him on, Mole coaxed and encouraged him, and the Rat went so far as to take him by the shoulders and shake him; but nothing could overcome his stage fright. They were all busily engaged on him like watermen applying the Royal Humane Society's regulations to a case of long submersion, when the latch clicked, the door opened, and the field mouse with the lantern reappeared, staggering under the weight of his basket.

There was no more talk of play-acting once the very real and solid contents of the basket had been tumbled out on the table. Under the generalship of Rat, everybody was set to do something or to fetch something. In a very few minutes supper was ready, and Mole, as he took the head of the table in a sort of dream, saw a lately barren board set thick with savory comforts; saw his little friends' faces brighten and beam as they fell to without delay; and then let himself loose—for he was famished indeed—on the provender so magically provided, thinking what a happy home-coming this had turned out, after all. As they ate, they talked of old times, and the field mice gave him the local gossip up to date, and answered as well as they could the hundred questions he had to ask them. The Rat said little or nothing, only taking care that each guest had what he wanted, and plenty of it, and that Mole had no trouble or anxiety about anything.

They clattered off at last, very grateful and showering wishes of the season, with their jacket pockets stuffed with remembrances for the small brothers and sisters at home. When the door had closed on the last of them and the chink of the lanterns had died away, Mole and Rat kicked the fire up, drew their chairs in, and discussed the events of the long day. At last the Rat, with a tremendous yawn, said, "Mole, old chap, I'm ready to drop. Sleepy is simply not the word. That your own bunk over on that side? Very well, then, I'll take this. What a ripping little house this is! Everything so handy!"

He clambered into his bunk and rolled himself well up in the blankets, and slumber gathered him forthwith, as a swath of barley is folded into the arms of the reaping machine.

The weary Mole also was glad to turn in without delay, and soon had his head on his pillow, in great joy and contentment. But ere he closed his eyes he let them wander round his old room, mellow in the glow of the firelight that played or rested on familiar and friendly things which had long been unconsciously a part of him, and now smilingly received him back, without rancor. He was now in just the frame of mind that the tactful Rat had quietly worked to bring about in him. He saw clearly how plain and simple—how narrow, even—it all was; but clearly, too, how much it all meant to him, and the special value of some such anchorage in one's existence. He did not at all want to abandon the new life and its splendid spaces, to turn his back on sun and air and all they offered him and creep home and stay there; the upper world was all too strong, it called to him still, even down there, and he knew he must return to the larger stage. But it was good to think he had this to come back to, this place which was all his own, these things which were so glad to see him again and could always be counted upon for the same simple welcome.

from *The Wind in the Willows*

Mr. Pickwick on the Ice

— 🍃 —

CHARLES DICKENS

"Now," said Wardle, after a substantial lunch, with the agreeable items of strong-beer and cherry-brandy, had been done ample justice to; "what say you to an hour on the ice? We shall have plenty of time."

"Capital!" said Mr. Benjamin Allen.

"Prime!" ejaculated Mr. Bob Sawyer.

"You skate, of course, Winkle?" said Wardle.

"Ye-yes; oh, yes," replied Mr. Winkle. "I—I am rather out of practice."

"Oh, do skate, Mr. Winkle," said Arabella. "I like to see it so much."

"Oh, it is so graceful," said another young lady.

A third young lady said it was elegant, and a fourth expressed her opinion that it was "swanlike."

"I should be very happy, I'm sure," said Mr. Winkle, reddening; "but I have no skates."

This objection was at once overruled. Trundle had a couple of pair, and the fat boy announced that there were half-a-dozen more downstairs; whereat Mr. Winkle expressed exquisite delight, and looked exquisitely uncomfortable.

Old Wardle led the way to a pretty large sheet of ice, and the fat boy and Mr. Weller, having shoveled and swept away the snow which had fallen on it during the night, Mr. Bob Sawyer adjusted his skates with a dexterity which to Mr. Winkle was perfectly marvelous, and described circles with his left leg, and cut figures of eight, and inscribed upon the ice, without once stopping for breath, a great many other pleasant and astonishing devices, to the excessive satisfaction of Mr. Pickwick, Mr. Tupman, and the ladies: which reached a pitch of positive enthusiasm, when old Wardle and Benjamin Allen, assisted by the aforesaid Bob Sawyer, performed some mystic evolutions, which they called a reel.

All this time, Mr. Winkle, with his face and hands blue with the cold, had been forcing a gimlet into the soles of his feet, and putting his skates on, with the points behind, and getting the straps into a very complicated and entangled state, with the assistance of Mr. Snodgrass, who knew rather less about skates than a Hindu. At length, however, with the assistance of Mr. Weller, the unfortunate skates were firmly screwed and buckled on, and Mr. Winkle was raised to his feet.

"Now, then, sir," said Sam, in an encouraging tone; "off vith you, and show 'em how to do it."

"Stop, Sam, stop!" said Mr. Winkle, trembling violently, and clutching hold of Sam's arms with the grasp of a drowning man. "How slippery it is, Sam!"

"Not an uncommon thing upon ice, sir," replied Mr. Weller. "Hold up, sir!"

This last observation of Mr. Weller's bore reference to a demonstration Mr. Winkle made at the instant, of a frantic desire to throw his feet in the air, and dash the back of his head on the ice.

"These—these—are very awkward skates; ain't they, Sam?" inquired Mr. Winkle, staggering.

"I'm afeerd there's a orkard gen'l'm'n in 'em, sir," replied Sam.

"Now, Winkle," cried Mr. Pickwick, quite unconscious that there was anything the matter. "Come; the ladies are all anxiety."

"Yes, yes," replied Mr. Winkle, with a ghastly smile; "I'm coming."

"Just a-goin' to begin," said Sam, endeavoring to disengage himself.

"Stop an instant, Sam," gasped Mr. Winkle, clinging most affectionately to Mr. Weller. "I find I've got a couple of coats at home that I don't want, Sam. You may have them, Sam."

"Thank'ee, sir," replied Mr. Weller.

"Never mind touching your hat, Sam," said Mr. Winkle, hastily; "you needn't take your hand away to do that. I meant to have given you five shillings this morning for a Christmas box, Sam. I'll give it you this afternoon, Sam."

"You're wery good, sir," replied Mr. Weller.

"Just hold me at first, Sam; will you?" said Mr. Winkle. "There—that's right. I shall soon get in the way of it, Sam. Not too fast, Sam; not too fast."

Mr. Winkle, stooping forward with his body half doubled up, was being assisted over the ice by Mr. Weller, in a very singular and un-swanlike manner, when Mr. Pickwick most innocently shouted from the opposite bank:

"Sam!"

"Sir?" said Mr. Weller.

"Here. I want you."

"Let go, sir," said Sam. "Don't you hear the governor a-callin'? Let go, sir."

With a violent effort, Mr. Weller disengaged himself from the grasp of the agonized Pickwickian, and in so doing administered a considerable impetus to the unhappy Mr. Winkle. With an accuracy which no degree of dexterity or practice could have insured, that unfortunate gentleman bore swiftly down into the center of the reel, at the very moment when Mr. Bob Sawyer was performing a flourish of unparalleled beauty. Mr. Winkle struck wildly against him, and with a loud crash they both fell heavily down. Mr. Pickwick ran to the spot. Bob Sawyer had risen to his feet, but Mr. Winkle was far too wise to do anything of the kind, in skates. He was seated on the ice, making spasmodic efforts to smile; but anguish was depicted on every lineament of his countenance.

"Are you hurt?" inquired Mr. Benjamin Allen, with great anxiety.

"Not much," said Mr. Winkle, rubbing his back very hard.

"I wish you'd let me bleed you," said Mr. Benjamin, with great eagerness.

"No, thank you," replied Mr. Winkle, hurriedly.

"I really think you had better," said Allen.

"Thank you," replied Mr. Winkle, "I'd rather not."

"What do you think, Mr. Pickwick?" inquired Bob Sawyer.

Mr. Pickwick was excited and indignant. He beckoned to Mr. Weller, and said, in a stern voice, "Take his skates off."

"No; but really I had scarcely begun," remonstrated Mr. Winkle.

"Take his skates off," repeated Mr. Pickwick firmly.

The command was not to be resisted. Mr. Winkle allowed Sam to obey in silence.

"Lift him up," said Mr. Pickwick. Sam assisted him to rise.

Mr. Pickwick retired a few paces apart from the bystanders,

and, beckoning his friend to approach, fixed a searching look upon him, and uttered in a low, but distinct and emphatic tone, these remarkable words:

"You're a humbug, sir."

"A what?" said Mr. Winkle, starting.

"A humbug, sir. I will speak plainer, if you wish it. An impostor, sir."

With those words Mr. Pickwick turned slowly on his heel, and rejoined his friends.

While Mr. Pickwick was delivering himself of the sentiment just recorded, Mr. Weller and the fat boy, having by their joint endeavors cut out a slide, were exercising themselves thereupon in a very masterly and brilliant manner. Sam Weller, in particular, was displaying that beautiful feat of fancy sliding which is currently denominated "knocking at the cobbler's door," and which is achieved by skimming over the ice on one foot, and occasionally giving a postman's knock upon it with the other. It was a good long slide, and there was something in the motion which Mr. Pickwick, who was very cold with standing still, could not help envying.

"It looks nice warm exercise that, doesn't it?" he inquired of Wardle, when that gentleman was thoroughly out of breath by reason of the indefatigable manner in which he had converted his legs into a pair of compasses, and drawn complicated problems on the ice.

"Ah, it does indeed," replied Wardle. "Do you slide?"

"I used to do so, on the gutters, when I was a boy," replied Mr. Pickwick.

"Try it now," said Wardle.

"Oh, do, please, Mr. Pickwick!" cried all the ladies.

"I should be very happy to afford you any amusement," replied Mr. Pickwick, "but I haven't done such a thing these thirty years."

"Pooh! pooh! Nonsense!" said Wardle, dragging off his skates with the impetuosity which characterized all his proceedings. "Here; I'll keep you company; come along!" And away went the good tempered old fellow down the slide, with a rapidity which came very close upon Mr. Weller, and beat the fat boy all to nothing.

Mr. Pickwick paused, considered, pulled off his gloves and put them in his hat; took two or three short runs, balked himself as often, and at last took another run, and went slowly and gravely down the slide, with his feet about a yard and a quarter apart, amidst the gratified shouts of all the spectators.

"Keep the pot a-bilin', sir!" said Sam; and down went Wardle again, and then Mr. Pickwick, and then Sam, and then Mr. Winkle, and then Mr. Bob Sawyer, and then the fat boy, and then Mr. Snodgrass, following closely upon each other's heels, and running after each other with as much eagerness as if all their future prospects in life depended on their expedition.

It was the most intensely interesting thing, to observe the manner in which Mr. Pickwick performed his share in the ceremony; to watch the torture of anxiety with which he viewed the person behind, gaining upon him at the imminent hazard of tripping him up; to see him gradually expend the painful force which he had put on at first, and turn slowly around on the slide, with his face towards the point from which he had started; to contemplate the playful smile which mantled on his face when he had accomplished the distance, and the eagerness with which he turned around when he had done so and ran after his predecessor; his black gaiters tripping pleasantly through the snow, and his eyes beaming cheerfulness and gladness through his spectacles. And when he was knocked down (which happened upon the average every third round), it was the most invigorating sight that can possibly be imagined, to behold him gather up his hat, gloves, and handkerchief, with a glowing countenance, and resume his station in the rank, with an ardor and enthusiasm that nothing could abate.

The sport was at its height, the sliding was at the quickest, the laughter was at the loudest, when a sharp smart crack was heard. There was a quick rush toward the bank, a wild scream from the ladies, and a shout from Mr. Tupman. A large mass of ice disappeared; the water bubbled over it; Mr. Pickwick's hat, gloves, and handkerchief were floating on the surface; and this was all of Mr. Pickwick that anybody could see.

Dismay and anguish were depicted on every countenance; the males turned pale, and the females fainted; Mr. Snodgrass and Mr. Winkle grasped each other by the hand, and gazed at the spot where their leader had gone down, with frenzied eagerness; while Mr. Tupman, by way of rendering the promptest assistance, and at the same time conveying to any persons who might be within hearing, the clearest possible notion of the catastrophe, ran off across the country at his utmost speed, screaming "Fire!" with all his might.

It was at this moment, when old Wardle and Sam Weller were approaching the hole with cautious steps, and Mr. Benjamin Allen was holding a hurried consultation with Mr. Bob Sawyer on the advisability of bleeding the company generally, as an improving little bit of professional practice—it was at this very moment that a face, head, and shoulders emerged from beneath the water, and disclosed the features and spectacles of Mr. Pickwick.

"Keep yourself up for an instant—for only one instant!" bawled Mr. Snodgrass.

"Yes, do; let me implore you—for my sake!" roared Mr. Winkle deeply affected. The adjuration was rather unnecessary; the probability being that if Mr. Pickwick had declined to keep himself up for anybody else's sake, it would have occurred to him that he might as well do so for his own.

"Do you feel the bottom there, old fellow?" said Wardle.

"Yes, certainly," replied Mr. Pickwick, wringing the water from his head and face, and gasping for breath. "I fell upon my back. I couldn't get on my feet at first."

The clay upon so much of Mr. Pickwick's coat as was yet visible bore testimony to the accuracy of this statement; and as the fears of the spectators were still further relieved by the fat boy's suddenly recollecting that the water was nowhere more than five feet deep, prodigies of valor were performed to get him out. After a vast quantity of splashing, and cracking, and struggling, Mr. Pickwick was at length fairly extricated from his unpleasant position, and once more stood on dry land.

"Oh, he'll catch his death of cold," said Emily.

"Dear old thing!" said Arabella. "Let me wrap this shawl around you, Mr. Pickwick."

"Ah, that's the best thing you can do," said Wardle; "and when you've got it on, run home as fast as your legs can carry you, and jump into bed directly."

A dozen shawls were offered on the instant. Three or four of the thickest having been selected, Mr. Pickwick was wrapped up, and started off, under the guidance of Mr. Weller; presently the singular phenomenon of an elderly gentleman, dripping wet, and without a hat, with his arms bound down to his sides, skimming over the ground, without any clearly defined purpose, at the rate of six good English miles an hour.

But Mr. Pickwick cared not for appearances in such an extreme case, and urged on by Sam Weller, he kept at the very top of his speed until he reached the door of Manor Farm, where Mr. Tupman had arrived some five minutes before, and had frightened the old lady into palpitations of the heart by impressing her with the unalterable conviction that the kitchen chimney was on fire—a calamity which always presented itself in glowing colors to the old lady's mind when anybody about her evinced the smallest agitation.

Mr. Pickwick paused not an instant until he was snug in bed.

from *The Pickwick Papers*

The Night Before Christmas

CLEMENT CLARKE MOORE

'Twas the night before Christmas, when all through the house,
Not a creature was stirring, not even a mouse.
The stockings were hung by the chimney with care,
In hopes that St. Nicholas soon would be there.
The children were nestled all snug in their beds,
While visions of sugarplums danced in their heads;
And Mama in her kerchief, and I in my cap,
Had just settled our brains for a long winter's nap,
When out on the lawn there arose such a clatter,
I sprang from my bed to see what was the matter.

Away to the window I flew like a flash,
Tore open the shutters and threw up the sash.
The moon on the breast of the new-fallen snow
Gave the luster of midday to objects below;
When what to my wondering eyes should appear,
But a miniature sleigh and eight tiny reindeer,
With a little old driver, so lively and quick,
I knew in a moment it must be St. Nick!

More rapid than eagles his coursers they came,
And he whistled and shouted and called them by name:
"Now, Dasher! now, Dancer! now, Prancer and Vixen!
On, Comet! on, Cupid! on, Donder and Blitzen!
To the top of the porch! to the top of the wall!
Now dash away! dash away! dash away, all!"

As dry leaves that before the wild hurricane fly,
When they meet with an obstacle, mount to the sky,
So up to the housetop the coursers they flew,
With the sleigh full of toys, and St. Nicholas, too.
And then in a twinkling I heard on the roof
The prancing and pawing of each little hoof.
As I drew in my head and was turning around,
Down the chimney St. Nicholas came with a bound.

He was dressed all in fur, from his head to his foot,
And his clothes were all tarnished with ashes and soot;
A bundle of toys he had flung on his back,
And he looked like a peddler just opening his pack.
His eyes how they twinkled! his dimples how merry!
His cheeks were like roses, his nose like a cherry!
His droll little mouth was drawn up like a bow,
And the beard on his chin was as white as the snow.

The stump of a pipe he held tight in his teeth,
And the smoke it encircled his head like a wreath.
He had a broad face and a little round belly
That shook, when he laughed, like a bowl full of jelly.
He was chubby and plump, a right jolly old elf,
And I laughed when I saw him, in spite of myself.
A wink of his eye and a twist of his head
Soon gave me to know I had nothing to dread.

He spoke not a word, but went straight to his work,
And filled all the stockings, then turned with a jerk,
And laying his finger aside of his nose,
And giving a nod, up the chimney he rose.
He sprang to his sleigh, to his team gave a whistle,
And away they all flew like the down of a thistle.
But I heard him exclaim, ere he drove out of sight,
"Happy Christmas to all, and to all a good night!"

The Nutcracker

A long time ago, in a land not so very far away, lived a little girl named Marie. Marie loved to play games and dance and draw pretty pictures. But, most of all—more than anything else—Marie loved Christmas.

One year, on Christmas Eve, Marie's father and mother had a party. Everyone in the village was there. There was music and dancing and all sorts of games and magic tricks. A huge tree filled the room and glittered with sparkling lights and tinsel.

Beneath the tree, in all shapes and colors, were the presents. When the time came to open them, the children quickly tore away the bright paper. What treasures they found! There were shiny brass trumpets and big fuzzy bears; lovely china dolls and bright tin soldiers. It was truly a wonderful Christmas.

And yet, the most wonderful part was still to come. Marie had a godfather. His name was Herr Drosselmeyer. Herr Drosselmeyer was a very unusual man. He wore a black patch over his right eye, and his long white hair stuck out wildly from his head. And Herr Drosselmeyer also had a very special skill—he was an excellent toymaker! This Christmas, Herr Drosselmeyer was bringing a special present just for Marie.

All the other gifts had already been opened. The guests were eating cakes and candies. The children were playing with their new toys.

When Herr Drosselmeyer suddenly appeared, the children were afraid—all except Marie. Happily, she ran to give him a hug. And then, he presented her with the best present of all.

"What did you get?"

The children crowded around as Marie quickly opened the small box.

"Ooooh," sighed Marie. "What a lovely little man."

The little man was a Nutcracker. He was dressed as a soldier. His mouth opened and closed. And his teeth were strong enough to crack the hardest of nuts.

"He looks so real," cried the children. It was true. The Nutcracker *did* look real. And yet, he was only made of wood.

Then something awful happened. Fritz, Marie's brother, grabbed the Nutcracker and ran off. Marie took off after him. In the excitement, Fritz dropped the little man.

"Oh, no," cried Marie. "He's broken."

Sure enough, the little Nutcracker's jaw had snapped. Marie was heartbroken.

"Come now, my child," said Herr Drosselmeyer. "He'll be all right. See, I'll just wrap my handkerchief around his head to keep his mouth shut. Don't worry. He'll be as good as new in the morning."

With that, the old man scooped up the broken toy. He placed

it in a tiny bed—just the right size for a Nutcracker. Marie sniffled a bit more, but she felt better. Somehow, she knew Herr Drosselmeyer was right.

As the hour grew late, the guests said good night. And one by one, they left. Marie went upstairs to bed. So did her parents and her brother Fritz. The house became quite still.

But Marie couldn't sleep. Silently, she tiptoed down the stairs to take another peek at her Nutcracker. Marie began to feel a bit uneasy. It was dark downstairs, and very quiet and still. The tree looked so big. And the toys looked so real....

Just then the clock struck midnight. Quickly, Marie turned around. And there, perched on top of the clock was an owl. And somehow, the owl looked very much like Herr Drosselmeyer.

Marie didn't have much time to wonder about this. All sorts of strange things were happening at once. The Christmas tree grew taller and taller. The room grew larger. And the toys, scattered about the tree, began to move. The soldiers and the dolls—and even the Nutcracker—were all coming to life!

Marie could hardly believe her eyes. But that wasn't all. She heard strange squeaks and creaks and rustling noises. Suddenly, an army of giant gray mice appeared. Now Marie was really frightened.

The Nutcracker quickly sprang into action. He grabbed a toy sword and led his army of tin soldiers against the mice. It was a fierce battle. The tin soldiers fought bravely. And so did the mice.

Screeeech! Marie heard a sharp whistle. The battle stopped. Everyone turned to see what the noise was. And there, at the foot of the tree, was the most curious creature Marie had ever seen.

It was a giant mouse—much bigger than any of the others. And, instead of one head, it had seven...each wearing a tiny golden crown. This was the Mouse King.

The Mouse King challenged the Nutcracker to a duel. What a horrible sight! The Nutcracker fought as best he could. But the ugly beast seemed to be everywhere at once. Finally, the Nutcracker fell to the ground. And the Mouse King was just about to pounce on him.

Terrified, Marie threw her slipper at the Mouse King. He was furious, and now he came after Marie. The poor girl was so frightened, she fainted. In that same instant, the Nutcracker bravely killed the Mouse King with his sword. The battle was over.

Proudly, the Nutcracker held one of the Mouse King's golden crowns above his head. As he did this, the little wooden man changed into a handsome young Prince. At once, everything else began to change, too.

The mice and the toys disappeared. Snow began to fall in great swirling gusts. And, before she knew what was happening, Marie was sailing through space with the Prince.

"Don't be frightened," he told her. "You saved my life. And now I am taking you to see the Kingdom of Sweets."

And so Marie began the most wonderful adventure of all. She and the Prince landed in a beautiful forest. Its trees were filled with thousands of tiny white candles. Lovely ripe fruit hung from all the branches.

"This is the Christmas Forest," said the Prince.

Next, they sailed together in a walnut shell down the River of Lemonade. All along the shore were houses made of candy. The roofs were covered with sugar icing, and the chimneys were made of jelly beans.

"This is all part of the magic land ruled by the Sugar Plum Fairy," explained the Prince.

As he spoke, they came to a magnificent palace. It was made completely of spun sugar. Just then, the Sugar Plum Fairy appeared. She was delighted to see them.

"Come inside," she said. After she had heard the story of their battle with the Mouse King, she said, "We shall celebrate your victory."

Inside the palace, tables were filled with every kind of sweet. There were chocolates and nougats and bonbons of all sizes and flavors. And then, the Sugar Plum Fairy danced for them. What a wonderful dance it was. Marie and the Prince joined in. And, finally, all the sweets and bonbons got up and danced with them.

Marie wished she could stay forever. But soon it was time to leave. A lovely white sleigh appeared. It was pulled by magic reindeer. As Marie and the Prince climbed in, the reindeer flew into the sky. Marie waved good-bye to the dancing Kingdom of Sweets. And away she sailed into the snowy night.

Marie climbed higher and higher into the sky. The snow grew thicker and thicker. Everything was white, and Marie felt so sleepy....

On Christmas morning, Marie awoke. There she was in her very own bed. Christmas—the day she loved more than any other—had finally come. Quickly, Marie raced downstairs to see the tree.

And there, in his own little bed, lay the Nutcracker. He was just as she had left him—only he wasn't broken anymore. He was as good as new—just as Herr Drosselmeyer had promised. What a wonderful Christmas surprise!

The Thieves Who Couldn't Help Sneezing

THOMAS HARDY

Many years ago, when oak trees now past their prime were about as large as elderly gentlemen's walking sticks, there lived in Wessex a yeoman's son, whose name was Hubert. He was about fourteen years of age, and was as remarkable for his candor and lightness of heart as for his physical courage, of which, indeed, he was a little vain.

One cold Christmas Eve his father, having no other help at hand, sent him on an important errand to a small town several miles from home. He traveled on horseback, and was detained by the business till a late hour of the evening. At last, however, it was completed; he returned to the inn, the horse was saddled, and he started on his way. His journey homeward lay through the Vale of Blackmore, a fertile but somewhat lonely district, with heavy clay roads and crooked lanes. In those days, too, a great part of it was thickly wooded.

It must have been about nine o'clock when, riding along amid the overhanging trees upon his stout-legged cob, Jerry, and singing a Christmas carol, to be in harmony with the season, Hubert fancied that he heard a noise among the boughs. This recalled to his mind that the spot he was traversing bore an evil name. Men had been waylaid there. He looked at Jerry, and wished he had been of any other color than light gray; for on this account the docile animal's form was visible even here in the dense shade. "What do I care?" he said aloud, after a few minutes reflection. "Jerry's legs are too nimble to allow any highwayman to come near me."

"Ha! ha! indeed," was said in a deep voice; and the next moment a man darted from the thicket on his right hand, another man from the thicket on his left hand, and another from a tree trunk a few yards ahead. Hubert's bridle was seized, he was pulled from his horse, and although he struck out with all his might, as a brave boy would naturally do, he was overpowered. His arms were tied behind him, his legs bound tightly together, and he was thrown into a ditch. The robbers, whose faces he could now dimly perceive to be artificially blackened, at once departed, leading off the horse.

As soon as Hubert had a little recovered himself, he found that by great exertion he was able to extricate his legs from the cord; but, in spite of every endeavor, his arms remained bound as fast as before. All, therefore, that he could do was to rise to his feet and proceed on his way with his arms behind him, and trust to chance for getting them unfastened. He knew that it would be impossible to reach home on foot that night, and in such a condition; but he walked on. Owing to the confusion which this attack caused in his brain, he lost his way, and would have been inclined to lie down and rest till morning among the dead leaves had he not known the danger of sleeping without wrappers in a frost so severe. So he wandered farther onward, his arms wrung and numbed by the cord which pinioned him, and his heart aching for the loss of poor Jerry, who never had been known to kick, or bite, or show a single vicious habit. He was not a little glad when he discerned through the trees a distant light. Towards this he made his way, and presently found himself in front of a large mansion with flanking wings, gables, and towers, the battlements and chimneys showing their shapes against the stars.

All was silent; but the door stood wide open, it being from this door that the light shone which had attracted him. On entering he found himself in a vast apartment arranged as a dining hall, and brilliantly illuminated. The walls were covered with a great deal of dark wainscoting, formed in panels, carvings, closet doors, and the usual fittings of a house of that kind. But what drew his attention was the table in the midst of the hall, upon which was spread a sumptuous supper, as yet untouched. Chairs were placed around, and it appeared as if something had occurred to interrupt the meal just at the time when all were ready to begin.

Even had Hubert been so inclined, he could not have eaten in his helpless state, unless by dipping his mouth into the dishes, like a pig or cow. He wished first to obtain assistance; and was about to penetrate farther into the house for that purpose when he heard hasty footsteps in the porch and the words, "Be quick!" uttered in the deep voice which had reached him when he was dragged from the horse. There was only just time for him to dart under the table before three men entered the dining hall. Peeping from beneath the hanging edges of the tablecloth, he perceived that their faces, too, were blackened, which at once removed any doubts he may have felt that these were the same thieves.

"Now, then," said the first—the man with the deep voice—"let us hide ourselves. They will all be back again in a minute. That was a good trick to get them out of the house—eh?"

"Yes. You well imitated the cries of a man in distress," said the second.

"Excellently," said the third.

"But they will soon find out that it was a false alarm. Come, where shall we hide? It must be some place we can stay in for two or three hours, till all are asleep. Ah! I have it. Come this way! I have learned that the farther cupboard is not opened once in a twelvemonth; it will serve our purpose exactly."

The speaker advanced into a corridor which led from the hall. Creeping a little farther forward, Hubert could discern that the cupboard stood at the end, facing the dining hall. The thieves entered it, and closed the door. Hardly breathing, Hubert glided forward, to learn a little more of their intention, if possible; and, coming close, he could hear the robbers whispering about the different rooms where the jewels, plate, and other valuables of the house were kept, which they plainly meant to steal.

They had not been long in hiding when a gay chattering of ladies and gentlemen was audible on the terrace without. Hubert felt that it would not do to be caught prowling about the house, unless he wished to be taken for a robber himself, and stood in a dark corner of the porch, where he could see everything without being himself seen. In a moment or two a whole troop of personages came gliding past him into the house. There were an elderly gentleman and lady, eight or nine young ladies, as many young men, besides half a dozen menservants and maids. The mansion had apparently been quite emptied of its occupants.

"Now, children and young people, we will resume our meal,"

said the old gentleman. "What the noise could have been I cannot understand. I never felt so certain in my life that there was a person being murdered outside my door."

Then the ladies began saying how frightened they had been, and how they had expected an adventure, and how it had ended in nothing after all.

"Wait a while," said Hubert to himself. "You'll have adventure enough by-and-by, ladies."

It appeared that the young men and women were married sons and daughters of the old couple, who had come that day to spend Christmas with their parents.

The door was then closed, Hubert being left outside in the porch. He thought this a proper moment for asking their assistance; and, since he was unable to knock with his hands, began boldly to kick the door.

"Hullo! What disturbance are you making here?" said a footman who opened it; and, seizing Hubert by the shoulder, he pulled him into the dining hall. "Here's a strange boy I have found making a noise in the porch, Sir Simon."

Everybody turned.

"Bring him forward," said Sir Simon, the old gentleman before mentioned. "What were you doing there, my boy?"

"Why, his arms are tied!" said one of the ladies.

"Poor fellow!" said another.

Hubert at once began to explain that he had been waylaid on his journey home, robbed of his horse, and mercilessly left in this condition by the thieves.

"Only to think of it!" exclaimed Sir Simon.

"That's a likely story," said one of the gentlemen-guests, incredulously.

"Doubtful, hey?" asked Sir Simon.

"Perhaps he's a robber himself," suggested a lady.

"There is a curiously wild wicked look about him, certainly, now that I examine him closely," said the old mother.

Hubert blushed with shame; and, instead of continuing his story, and relating that robbers were concealed in the house, he doggedly held his tongue, and half resolved to let them find out their danger for themselves.

"Well, untie him," said Sir Simon. "Come, since it is Christmas Eve, we'll treat him well. Here, my lad; sit down in that empty seat at the bottom of the table, and make as good a meal as you can. When you have had your fill we will listen to more particulars of your story."

The feast then proceeded; and Hubert, now at liberty, was not at all sorry to join in. The more they ate and drank the merrier did the company become; the wine flowed freely, the logs flared up the chimney, the ladies laughed at the gentlemen's stories; in short, all went as noisily and as happily as a Christmas gathering in old times possibly could do.

Hubert, in spite of his hurt feelings at their doubts of his honesty, could not help being warmed both in mind and in body by the good cheer, the scene, and the example of hilarity set by his neighbors. At last he laughed as heartily at their stories and repartees as the old Baronet, Sir Simon, himself. When the meal was almost over one of the sons, who had drunk a little too much wine, after the manner of men in that century, said to Hubert, "Well, my boy, can you take a pinch of snuff?" He held out one of the snuffboxes which were then becoming common among young and old throughout the country.

"Thank you," said Hubert, accepting a pinch.

"Tell the ladies who you are, what you are made of, and what you can do," the young man continued, slapping Hubert upon the shoulder.

"Certainly," said our hero, drawing himself up, and thinking it best to put a bold face on the matter. "I am a traveling magician."

"Indeed!"

"What shall we hear next?"

"Can you call up spirits from the vasty deep, young wizard?"

"I can conjure up a tempest in a cupboard," Hubert replied.

"Ha-ha!" said the old Baronet, pleasantly rubbing his hands. "We must see this performance. Girls, don't go away: here's something to be seen."

"Not dangerous, I hope?" said the old lady.

Hubert rose from the table. "Hand me your snuffbox, please," he said to the young man who had made free with him. "And now," he continued, "without the least noise, follow me. If you speak it will break the spell."

They promised obedience. He entered the corridor, and, taking off his shoes, went on tiptoe to the cupboard door, the guests advancing in a silent group at a little distance behind him. Hubert next placed a stool in front of the door, and, by standing upon it, was tall enough to reach the top. He then poured all the snuff from the box along the upper edge of the door, and, with a few short puffs of breath, blew the snuff through the chink into the interior of the cupboard. He held up his finger to the assembly, that they might be silent.

"Dear me, what's that?" said the old lady, after a minute or two had elapsed.

A suppressed sneeze had come from inside the cupboard.

Hubert held up his finger again.

"How very singular," whispered Sir Simon. "This is most interesting."

Hubert took advantage of the moment to gently slide the bolt of the cupboard door into its place. "More snuff," he said, calmly.

"More snuff," said Sir Simon. Two or three gentlemen passed their boxes, and the contents were blown in at the top of the cupboard. Another sneeze, not quite so well suppressed as the first, was heard: then another, which seemed to say that it would not be suppressed under any circumstances whatever. At length there arose a perfect storm of sneezes.

"Excellent for one so young!" said Sir Simon. "I am much interested in this trick of throwing the voice—called, I believe, ventriloquism."

"More snuff," said Hubert.

"More snuff," said Sir Simon. Sir Simon's man brought a large jar of the best scented Scotch.

Hubert once more charged the upper chink of the cupboard, and blew the snuff into the interior, as before. Again he charged, and again, emptying the whole contents of the jar. The tumult of sneezes became really extraordinary to listen to—there was no cessation. It was like wind, rain, and sea battling in a hurricane.

"I believe there are men inside, and that it is no trick at all!" exclaimed Sir Simon, the truth flashing on him.

"There are," said Hubert. "They are come to rob the house; and they are the same who stole my horse."

The sneezes changed to spasmodic groans. One of the thieves, hearing Hubert's voice, cried, "Oh! mercy! mercy! let us out of this!"

"Where's my horse?" cried Hubert.

"Tied to the tree in the hollow behind Short's Gibbet. Mercy! mercy! let us out, or we shall die of suffocation!"

All the Christmas guests now perceived that this was no longer sport, but serious earnest. Guns and cudgels were procured; all the menservants were called in, and arranged in position outside the cupboard. At a signal Hubert withdrew the bolt, and stood on the defensive. But the three robbers, far from attacking them, were found crouching in the corner, gasping for breath. They made no resistance; and, being pinioned, were placed in an outhouse till morning.

Hubert now gave the remainder of his story to the assembled

company, and was profusely thanked for the services he had rendered. Sir Simon pressed him to stay over the night, and accept the use of the best bedroom the house afforded, which had been occupied by Queen Elizabeth and King Charles successively when on their visits to this part of the country. But Hubert declined, being anxious to find his horse Jerry, and to test the truth of the robbers' statements concerning him.

Several of the guests accompanied Hubert to the spot behind the gibbet, alluded to by the thieves as where Jerry was hidden. When they reached the knoll and looked over, behold! there the horse stood, uninjured, and quite unconcerned. At sight of Hubert he neighed joyfully: and nothing could exceed Hubert's gladness at finding him. He mounted, wished his friends "Good night!" and cantered off in the direction they pointed out, reaching home safely about four o'clock in the morning.

The Story of the Goblins Who Stole a Sexton

CHARLES DICKENS

In an old abbey town, down in this part of the country, a long, long while ago—so long, that the story must be a true one, because our great-grandfathers implicitly believed it—there officiated as sexton and gravedigger in the churchyard, one Gabriel Grub. It by no means follows that because a man is a sexton, and constantly surrounded by emblems of mortality, therefore he should be a morose and melancholy man; your undertakers are the merriest fellows in the world, and I once had the honor of being on intimate terms with a mute, who in private life, and off duty, was as comical and jocose a little fellow as ever chirped out a devil-may-care song, without a hitch in his memory, or drained off a good stiff glass of grog without stopping for breath. But notwithstanding these precedents to the contrary, Gabriel Grub was an ill-conditioned, cross-grained, surly fellow—a morose and lonely man, who consorted with nobody but himself, and an old wicker bottle which fitted into his large deep waistcoat pocket; and who eyed each merry face as it passed him by, with such a deep scowl of malice and ill-humor, as it was difficult to meet without feeling something the worse for.

A little before twilight one Christmas Eve, Gabriel shouldered his spade, lighted his lantern, and betook himself towards the old churchyard, for he had got a grave to finish by next morning, and feeling very low he thought it might raise his spirits perhaps, if he went on with his work at once. As he wended his way, up the ancient street, he saw the cheerful light of the blazing fires gleam through the old casements, and heard the loud laugh and the cheerful shouts of those who were assembled around them; he marked the bustling preparations for the next day's good cheer, and smelled the numerous savory odors consequent thereupon, as they steamed up from the kitchen windows in clouds. All this was gall and wormwood to the heart of Gabriel Grub; and as groups of children, bounded out of the houses, tripped across the road, and were met, before they could knock at the opposite door, by half a dozen curly-headed little rascals who crowded around them as they flocked up stairs to spend the evening in their Christmas games, Gabriel smiled grimly, and clutched the handle of his spade with a firmer grasp, as he thought of measles, scarlet-fever, thrush, whooping cough, and a good many other sources of consolation beside.

In this happy frame of mind, Gabriel strode along, returning a short, sullen growl to the good-humored greetings of such of his neighbors as now and then passed him, until he turned into the dark lane which led to the churchyard. Now Gabriel had been looking forward to reaching the dark lane, because it was, generally speaking, a nice gloomy mournful place, into which the townspeople did not care much to go, except in broad daylight, and when the sun was shining; consequently he was not a little indignant to hear a young urchin roaring out some jolly song about a merry Christmas, in this very sanctuary, which had been called Coffin Lane ever since the days of the old abbey, and the time of the shaven-headed monks. As Gabriel walked on, and the voice drew nearer, he found it proceeded from a small boy, who was hurrying along, to join one of the little parties in the old street, and who, partly to keep himself company, and partly to prepare himself for the occasion, was shouting out the song at the highest pitch of his lungs. So Gabriel waited till the boy came up, and then dodged him into a corner, and rapped him over the head with his lantern five or six times, just to teach him to modulate his voice. And as the boy hurried away with his hand to his head, singing quite a different sort of tune, Gabriel Grub chuckled very heartily to himself, and entered the churchyard, locking the gate behind him.

He took off his coat, set down his lantern, and getting into the unfinished grave, worked at it for an hour or so, with right good will. But the earth was hardened with the frost, and it was no very easy matter to break it up, and shovel it out; and although there was a moon, it was a very young one, and shed little light upon the grave, which was in the shadow of the church. At any other time, these obstacles would have made Gabriel Grub very moody and miserable, but he was so well pleased with having stopped the small boy's singing, that he took little heed of the scanty progress he had made, and looked down into the grave when he had finished work for the night, with grim satisfaction, murmuring as he gathered up his things—

Brave lodgings for one, brave lodgings for one,
A few feet of cold earth, when life is done;
A stone at the head, a stone at the feet,
A rich, juicy meal for the worms to eat;
Rank grass overhead, and damp clay around,
Brave lodgings for one, these, in holy ground!

"Ho! Ho!" laughed Gabriel Grub, as he sat himself down on a flat tombstone which was a favorite resting place of his; and drew forth his wicker bottle. "A coffin at Christmas—a Christmas Box. Ho! Ho! Ho!"

"Ho! Ho! Ho!" repeated a voice which sounded close behind him.

Gabriel paused in some alarm, in the act of raising the wicker bottle to his lips, and looked around. The bottom of the oldest grave about him, was not more still and quiet, than the churchyard in the pale moonlight. The cold hoar frost glistened on the tombstones, and sparkled like rows of gems among the stone carvings of the old church. The snow lay hard and crisp upon the ground, and spread over the thickly-strewn mounds of earth, so white and smooth a cover, that it seemed as if corpses lay there, hidden only by their winding sheets. Not the faintest rustle broke the profound tranquillity of the solemn scene. Sound itself appeared to be frozen up, all was so cold and still.

"It was the echoes," said Gabriel Grub, raising the bottle to his lips again.

"It was *not*," said a deep voice.

Gabriel started up, and stood rooted to the spot with astonishment and terror; for his eyes rested on a form which made his blood run cold.

Seated on an upright tombstone, close to him, was a strange unearthly figure, whom Gabriel felt at once, was no being of this world. His long fantastic legs which might have reached the ground, were cocked up, and crossed after a quaint, fantastic fashion; his sinewy arms were bare, and his hands rested on his knees. On his short round body he wore a close covering, ornamented with small slashes; and a short cloak dangled at his back; the collar was cut into curious peaks, which served the goblin in lieu of ruff or neckerchief; and his shoes curled up at the toes into long points. On his head he wore a broad-brimmed sugar-loaf hat, garnished with a single feather. The hat was covered with the white frost, and the goblin looked as if he had sat on the same tombstone very comfortably, for two or three hundred years. He was sitting perfectly still; his tongue was put out, as if in derision; and he was grinning at Gabriel Grub with such a grin as only a goblin could call up.

"It was *not* the echoes," said the goblin.

Gabriel Grub was paralyzed, and could make no reply.

"What do you do here on Christmas Eve?" said the goblin sternly.

"I came to dig a grave, Sir," stammered Gabriel Grub.

"What man wanders among the graves and churchyards on such a night as this?" said the goblin.

"Gabriel Grub! Gabriel Grub!" screamed a wild chorus of voices that seemed to fill the churchyard. Gabriel looked fearfully around—nothing was to be seen.

"What have you got in that bottle?" said the goblin.

"Hollands, Sir," replied the sexton, trembling more than ever; for he had bought it off the smugglers, and he thought that perhaps his questioner might be in the excise department of the goblins.

"Who drinks Hollands alone, and in a churchyard, on such a night as this?" said the goblin.

"Gabriel Grub! Gabriel Grub!" exclaimed the wild voices again.

The goblin leered maliciously at the terrified sexton, and then raising his voice, exclaimed—

"And who, then, is our fair and lawful prize?"

To this inquiry the invisible chorus replied, in a strain that sounded like the voices of many choristers singing to the mighty swell of the old church organ—a strain that seemed borne to the sexton's ears upon a gentle wind, and to die away as its soft breath passed onward—but the burden of the reply was still the same, "Gabriel Grub! Gabriel Grub!"

The goblin grinned a broader grin than before, as he said, "Well, Gabriel, what do you say to this?"

The sexton gasped for breath.

"What do you think of this, Gabriel?" said the goblin, kicking up his feet in the air on either side of the tombstone, and looking at the turned-up points with as much complacency as if he had been contemplating the most fashionable pair of Wellingtons in all Bond Street.

"It's—it's—very curious, Sir," replied the sexton, half dead with fright, "very curious, and very pretty, but I think I'll go back and finish my work, Sir, if you please."

"Work!" said the goblin, "what work?"

"The grave, Sir, making the grave," stammered the sexton.

"Oh, the grave, eh?" said the goblin, "who makes graves at a time when all other men are merry, and takes a pleasure in it?"

Again the mysterious voices replied, "Gabriel Grub! Gabriel Grub!"

"I'm afraid my friends want you, Gabriel," said the goblin, thrusting his tongue further into his cheek than ever—and a most astonishing tongue it was—"I'm afraid my friends want you, Gabriel," said the goblin.

"Under favor, Sir," replied the horror-struck sexton, "I don't think they can, Sir; they don't know me, Sir; I don't think the gentlemen have ever seen me, Sir."

"Oh yes they have," replied the goblin; "we know the man with the sulky face and the grim scowl, that came down the street tonight, throwing his evil looks at the children, and grasping his burying spade the tighter. We know the man that struck the boy in the envious malice of his heart, because the boy could be merry, and he could not. We know him, we know him."

Here the goblin gave a loud shrill laugh, that the echoes returned twenty-fold, and throwing his legs up in the air, stood upon his head, or rather upon the very point of his sugar-loaf hat, on the narrow edge of the tombstone, from whence he threw a summerset with extraordinary agility, right to the sexton's feet, at which he planted himself in the attitude in which tailors generally sit upon the shop-board.

"I—I—am afraid I must leave you, Sir," said the sexton, making an effort to move.

"Leave us!" said the goblin, "Gabriel Grub going to leave us. Ho! ho! ho!"

As the goblin laughed, the sexton observed for one instant a brilliant illumination within the windows of the church, as if the whole building were lighted up; it disappeared, the organ peeled forth a lively air, and whole troops of goblins, the very counterpart of the first one, poured into the churchyard, and began playing at leapfrog with the tombstones, never stopping for an instant to take breath, but overing the highest among them, one after the other, with the most marvelous dexterity. The first goblin was a most astonishing leaper, and none of the others could come near him; even in the extremity of his terror the sexton could not help observing, that while his friends were content to leap over the common-sized gravestones, the first one took the family vaults, iron railings and all, with as much ease as if they had been so many street posts.

At last the game reached to a most exciting pitch; the organ played quicker and quicker, and the goblins leaped faster and faster, coiling themselves up, rolling head over heels upon the ground, and bounding over the tombstones like footballs. The sexton's brain whirled around with the rapidity of the motion he beheld, and his legs reeled beneath him, as the spirits flew before his eyes, when the goblin king suddenly darting towards him, laid his hand upon his collar, and sank with him through the earth.

When Gabriel Grub had had time to fetch his breath, which the rapidity of his descent had for the moment taken away, he found himself in what appeared to be a large cavern, surrounded on all sides by crowds of goblins, ugly and grim; in the center of the room, on an elevated seat, was stationed his friend of the churchyard; and close beside him stood Gabriel Grub himself, without the power of motion.

"Cold tonight," said the king of the goblins, "very cold. A glass of something warm, here."

At this command, half a dozen officious goblins, with a perpetual smile upon their faces, whom Gabriel Grub imagined to be courtiers on that account, hastily disappeared, and presently returned with a goblet of liquid fire, which they presented to the king.

"Ah!" said the goblin, whose cheeks and throat were transparent, as he tossed down the flame, "this warms one, indeed: bring a bumper of the same, for Mr. Grub."

It was in vain for the unfortunate sexton to protest that he was not in the habit of taking anything warm at night; for one of the goblins held him while another poured the blazing liquid down his throat, and the whole assembly screeched with laughter as he coughed and choked, and wiped away the tears which gushed plentifully from his eyes, after swallowing the burning draught.

"And now," said the king, fantastically poking the taper corner of his sugar-loaf hat into the sexton's eye, and thereby occasioning him the most exquisite pain—"And now, show the man of misery and gloom a few of the pictures from our own great storehouse."

As the goblin said this, a thick cloud which obscured the further end of the cavern, rolled gradually away, and disclosed, apparently at a great distance, a small and scantily furnished, but neat and clean apartment. A crowd of little children were gathered around a bright fire, clinging to their mother's gown, and gamboling around her chair. The mother occasionally rose, and drew aside the window-curtain as if to look for some expected object; a frugal meal was ready spread upon the table, and an elbow chair was placed near the fire. A knock was heard at the door: the mother opened it, and the children crowded around her, and clapped their hands for joy, as their father entered. He was wet and weary, and shook the snow from his garments, as the children crowded around him, and seizing his cloak, hat, stick, and gloves, with busy zeal, ran with them from the room. Then as he sat down to his meal before the fire, the children climbed about his knee, and the mother sat by his side, and all seemed happiness and comfort.

But a change came upon the view, almost imperceptibly. The scene was altered to a small bedroom, where the fairest and youngest child lay dying; the roses had fled from his cheek, and the light from his eye; and even as the sexton looked upon him with an interest he had never felt or known before, he died. His young brothers and sisters crowded around his little bed, and seized his tiny hand, so cold and heavy; but they shrank back from its touch, and looked with awe on his infant face; for calm and tranquil as it was, and sleeping in rest and peace as the beautiful child seemed to be, they saw that he was dead, and they knew that he was an angel looking down upon, and blessing them, from a bright and happy Heaven.

Again the light cloud passed across the picture, and again the subject changed. The father and mother were old and helpless now, and the number of those about them was diminished more than half; but content and cheerfulness sat on every face, and beamed in every eye, as they crowded around the fireside, and told and listened to old stories of earlier and bygone days. Slowly and peacefully the father sank into the grave, and, soon after, the sharer of all his cares and troubles followed him to a place of rest and peace. The few, who yet survived them, knelt by their tomb, and watered the green turf which covered it with their tears; then rose and turned away, sadly and mournfully, but not with bitter cries, or despairing lamentations, for they knew that they should one day meet again; and once more they mixed with the busy world, and their content and cheerfulness was restored. The cloud settled upon the picture, and concealed it from the sexton's view.

"What do you think of *that*?" said the goblin, turning his large face towards Gabriel Grub.

Gabriel murmured out something about its being very pretty, and looked somewhat ashamed, as the goblin bent his fiery eyes upon him.

"*You* a miserable man!" said the goblin, in a tone of excessive contempt. "You!" He appeared disposed to add more, but indignation choked his utterance, so he lifted up one of his very pliable legs, and flourishing it above his head a little, to insure his aim, administered a good sound kick to Gabriel Grub; immediately after which, all the goblins in waiting crowded around the wretched sexton, and kicked him without mercy, according to the established and invariable custom of courtiers upon earth, who kick whom royalty kicks, and hug whom royalty hugs.

"Show him some more," said the king of the goblins.

At these words the cloud was again dispelled, and a rich and beautiful landscape was disclosed to view—there is just such another to this day, within half a mile of the old abbey town. The sun shone from out the clear blue sky, the water sparkled beneath his rays, and the trees looked greener, and the flowers more gay, beneath his cheering influence. The water rippled on, with a pleasant sound, the trees rustled in the light wind that murmured among their leaves, the birds sang upon the boughs, and the lark caroled on high, her welcome to the morning. Yes, it was morning, the bright, balmy morning of summer; the minutest leaf, the smallest blade of grass, was instinct with life. The ant crept forth to her daily toil, the butterfly fluttered and basked in the warm rays of the sun; myriads of insects spread their transparent wings, and reveled in their brief but happy existence. Man walked forth, elated with the scene; and all was brightness and splendor.

"*You* a miserable man!" said the king of goblins, in a more contemptuous tone than before. And again the king of the goblins gave his leg a flourish; again it descended on the shoulders of the sexton; and again the attendant goblins imitated the example of their chief.

Many a time the cloud went and came, and many a lesson it taught to Gabriel Grub, who although his shoulders smarted with pain from the frequent applications of the goblins' feet thereunto, looked on with an interest which nothing could diminish. He saw that men who worked hard, and earned their scanty bread with lives of labor, were cheerful and happy; and that to the most ignorant, the sweet face of nature was a never-failing source of cheerfulness and joy. He saw those who had been delicately nurtured, and tenderly brought up, cheerful under privations, and superior to suffering, that would have crushed many a rougher grain, because they bore within their own bosoms the materials of happiness, contentment, and peace. He saw that women, the tenderest and most fragile of all God's creatures, were the oftenest superior to sorrow, adversity, and distress; and he saw that it was because they bore in their own hearts an inexhaustible wellspring of affection and devotedness. Above all, he saw that men like himself, who snarled at the mirth and cheerfulness of others, were the foulest weeds on the fair surface of the earth; and settling all the good of the world against the evil, he came to the conclusion that it was a very decent and respectable sort of world after all. No sooner had he formed it, than the cloud which had closed over the last picture, seemed to settle on his senses, and lull him to repose. One by one, the goblins faded from his sight, and as the last one disappeared, he sunk to sleep.

The day had broken when Gabriel Grub awoke, and found himself lying at full length on the flat gravestone in the churchyard, with the wicker bottle lying empty by his side, and his coat, spade, and lantern, all well whitened by the last night's frost, scattered on the ground. The stone on which he had first seen the goblin seated, stood bolt upright before him, and the grave at which he had worked, the night before, was not far off. At first he began to doubt the reality of his adventures, but the acute pain in his shoulders when he attempted to rise, assured him that the kicking of the goblins was certainly not ideal. He was staggered again, by observing no traces of footsteps in the snow on which the goblins had played at leapfrog with the gravestones, but he speedily accounted for this circumstance when he remembered that being spirits, they would leave no visible impression behind them. So Gabriel Grub got to his feet as well as he could, for the pain in his back; and brushing the frost off his coat, put it on, and turned his face towards the town.

But he was an altered man, and he could not bear the thought of returning to a place where his repentance would be scoffed at, and his reformation disbelieved. He hesitated for a few moments; and then turned away to wander where he might, and seek his bread elsewhere.

The lantern, the spade, and the wicker bottle, were found that day in the churchyard. There were a great many speculations about the sexton's fate at first, but it was speedily determined that he had been carried away by the goblins; and there were not wanting some very credible witnesses who had distinctly seen him whisked through the air on the back of a chestnut horse blind of one eye, with the hind quarters of a lion, and the tail of a bear. At length all this was devoutly believed; and the new sexton used to exhibit to the curious for a trifling emolument, a good-sized piece of the church weathercock which had been accidentally kicked off by the aforesaid horse in his aerial flight, and picked up by himself in the churchyard, a year or two afterwards.

Unfortunately these stories were somewhat disturbed by the unlooked-for reappearance of Gabriel Grub himself, some ten years afterwards, a ragged, contented, rheumatic old man. He told his story to the clergyman, and also to the mayor; and in course of time it began to be received as a matter of history, in which form it has continued down to this very day. The believers in the weathercock tale, having misplaced their confidence once, were not easily prevailed upon to part with it again, so they looked as wise as they could, shrugged their shoulders, touched their foreheads, and murmured something about Gabriel Grub's having drunk all the Hollands, and then fallen asleep on the flat tombstone; and they affected to explain what he supposed he had witnessed in the goblins' cavern, by saying that he had seen the world, and grown wiser. But this opinion, which was by no means a popular one at any time, gradually died off, and be the matter how it may, as Gabriel Grub was affected with rheumatism to the end of his days, this story has at least one moral, if it teach no better one— and that is, that if a man turns sulky and drinks by himself at Christmas time, he may make up his mind to be not a bit the better for it, let the spirits be ever so good, or let them be even as many degrees beyond proof, as those which Gabriel Grub saw, in the goblins' cavern.

Baboushka

———— ❦ ————

O nce upon a time, in a little house deep in the forest, there lived an old woman called Baboushka. Although she lived all alone, Baboushka never felt lonely. She was always busy cooking, cleaning, sewing, or gathering wood, and as she worked she would sing to herself. The songs, old ones, as well as new ones she made up, kept her company through the day. It was many miles to the nearest town and a long way to her nearest neighbors, so Baboushka hardly ever had any visitors.

One day, however, in the middle of winter, she heard voices through the trees. The voices grew louder. They were coming toward her! Baboushka ran excitedly into the house. She put the kettle on the hob then hurried out to fetch some more logs for the fire. She had just brought them in when there was a loud knock at the door.

"Who is it?" called Baboushka.

"Three weary travelers, good woman," a voice answered. "We can't find our way through the forest and it is growing dark outside. Can you give us shelter so we can rest for a few minutes before going on our way?"

At once Baboushka flung open the door. "Come in," she beamed, "you are most welcome to rest yourself by the fire. Have some tea to warm you up."

One by one the travelers came in. First there was a young man, who smiled at her. Then he turned to help an older man, who looked very tired indeed. The last man was tall and fierce-looking, with shining gold rings in his ears. All three shook the snow from their rich, finely decorated clothes and sat around the fire. Baboushka made some good, strong tea for them and cut slices of bread. As she did so, she asked the men where they were going.

"We don't know," answered the young man. "It's all very strange. We are searching for a baby prince. His star has guided us all this way, but now the sky is so full of snow that we can't see it anymore."

"Don't worry," said Baboushka, not quite understanding. "When you've eaten, I'll show you where the road is, and then you won't need to follow a star!"

"You are very kind," the young man answered, "but only the star can lead us to the Christ child."

"A child and a star!" Baboushka was astonished. "What can this mean?"

Then the old man explained to her that the star was the sign of a holy child's birth, which had been sent to lead them. He showed Baboushka rich presents that they were taking to give the child when they found him.

Baboushka's eyes were glowing.

"I wish I could see this child," she murmured.

"Come with us," they cried, all together. "Help us in our search."

But Baboushka shook her head sadly. "I'm much too old to travel," she said, and she began pouring out the tea. When the three men had eaten and rested, they thanked her for her hospitality and set off again through the trees. The house seemed suddenly very empty. Baboushka sat in her rocking chair, rocking slowly with a thoughtful look on her face. Suddenly she jumped to her feet.

"I will!" she cried. "I will join the search! I'll go tomorrow, so I will!"

Quickly Baboushka packed a small bundle of clothes, then she collected all her greatest treasures to take as presents to the holy child; a wooden horse, an old doll, a cloth ball, a few painted fir cones, and some pretty feathers.

Early the next morning, she dressed in her warmest clothes and left her little house. She set off in the direction the travelers had gone, but fresh snow had quite covered all their tracks.

"Have three kings passed this way?" she asked a farmer.

"Kings! In this weather? What a foolish question," roared the farmer, and he stomped away crossly. Then she met a shepherd.

"Have you seen a bright star?" she asked him eagerly.

"Thousands," he chuckled. "Right above you. And they all shine brightly!"

A herdsman trudged past with his herd of cattle.

"Have any baby princes been born here lately?" Baboushka questioned him anxiously.

"We've plenty of babies," he replied, "but not a prince among them."

She tramped on wearily, stopping everyone she met to ask, "Have you seen the Christ child, please?" But no one could help her.

And to this very day, Baboushka has never stopped searching. She still travels her country looking for the baby prince. And whenever she meets with a child who is sick or unhappy, she digs deep into her pack and always finds a little toy to make them smile.